For my brothers, Derek and Christopher, who came with the
terror-tory – from Wendy with love.

For Jess who is learning to say 'Diplodocus' and other wonderful
words – from Niki with love.

MARGARET K. MCELDERRY BOOKS
25 YEARS • 1972–1997

Margaret K. McElderry Books
An imprint of Simon & Schuster Children's Publishing Division
1230 Avenue of the Americas
New York, New York 10020

Text copyright © 1996 by Wendy Hartmann and Niki Daly
Illustrations copyright © 1996 by Niki Daly

First published in London by the Bodley Head Children's Books

First United States edition, 1997

Printed in Hong Kong

10 9 8 7 6 5 4 3 2 1

Library of Congress Catalog Card Number: 96-77059

ISBN 0-689-81152-7

The DINOSAURS Are Back

And it's all your fault Edward!

Story by
Wendy Hartmann & Niki Daly
Pictures by Niki Daly

Margaret K. McElderry Books

"Edward?"

"*Mmmm?*"

"What if that rock under your bed isn't a rock at all...? What if it's an egg, Edward?"

"Huuuh!"

"What if it's a DINOSAUR EGG...?"

"... and it hatches, Edward?"

"It'll eat like a garbage truck."

"And SOMEBODY will have to change its diaper."

"It'll need potty-training, Edward."

"As it grows up you'll have to teach it good manners."

"And how to behave when Aunt Vi comes around."

"You'll have to take it for walks."

"What if it follows you to school, Edward?

And wants to go everywhere you go...

and do everything you do?

It'll be just like a shadow, Edward."

"You'll have to watch it every moment of the day…

and night, Edward."

"Dinosaurs sleep at night, stupid!"

"Edward, EDWARD!"

"What?"

"Not when there's a big, crazy moon.

"A big, crazy moon makes dinosaurs REALLY mad, Edward.

SO mad that they forget who their friends are."

"They run wild,
looking for their mother and father.

Hollering for their brothers and sisters...
cousins, aunts and uncles...
Howling for their big grandaddy...

"The King of the Dinosaurs."

"Then they go looking for little boys
who steal dinosaur eggs!"

"They drag the little egg-stealer, kicking and screaming, right out of bed!"